Shadow of Retribution

KAMRIN

S.H.E. PUBLISHING.LLC

SHADOW OF RETRIBUTION
Copyright © 2024 by Kamrin

For information contact :
info@shepublishingllc.com
www.shepublishingllc.com
ISBN :
978-1-953163-97-4
(hardback)
First Edition : February 2024

10 9 8 7 6 5 4 3 2 1

The cartel's leader, filled with rage, asked Bruce if he remembered his brother. When Bruce claimed ignorance, the leader ordered his men to subject his family to unimaginable acts of cruelty. Helpless, Bruce could only watch in tears of rage and sadness.

The men finished their heinous deeds, leaving Bruce's loved ones broken in pieces. Then, they bagged Bruce's head, leaving him unconscious once more. When he woke up, battered and disfigured, he found himself dumped near the docks, his body burned and scarred from the severe torture he endured.

A Flame Ignited

Bruce Butler Andrews was once a renowned MMA fighter, an English teacher and a former member of the special forces. However, his life took a devastating turn when he found himself tracked by a merciless cartel for killing the leader's brother.

One fateful night, they broke into Bruce's home, with hopes of serving revenge. He put up a fierce fight, but was eventually overpowered and knocked unconscious. Waking up to a horrifying scene, his wife and young son were bound and at the mercy of the cartel's men.

As fate would have it, his lifeless body was discovered by a clandestine experiment boat. Driven by their own twisted intentions, the scientists reanimated Bruce to hide his grotesque appearance, leaving him with bandages covering his mangled form.

A doctor by the name of Gott Schlous took a particular interest in Bruce's case, influencing him with dark motives. He persuaded Bruce to enact revenge on everyone present that night, leaving only one thing on Bruce's mind: vengeance.

Bruce embraced his new identity of darkness, becoming a vigilante with a single purpose. The pain inflicted upon him during his transformation had a peculiar side effect. His nerves, burnt and cauterized, left him without the ability to feel initial physical pain; however, Bruce could still be harmed and injured.

With his newfound resistance to pain and a heart consumed by revenge, Bruce Butler Andrews, now a fearsome antihero, sets out on a relentless mission to hunt down and punish those responsible for the horrors inflicted upon him and his family.

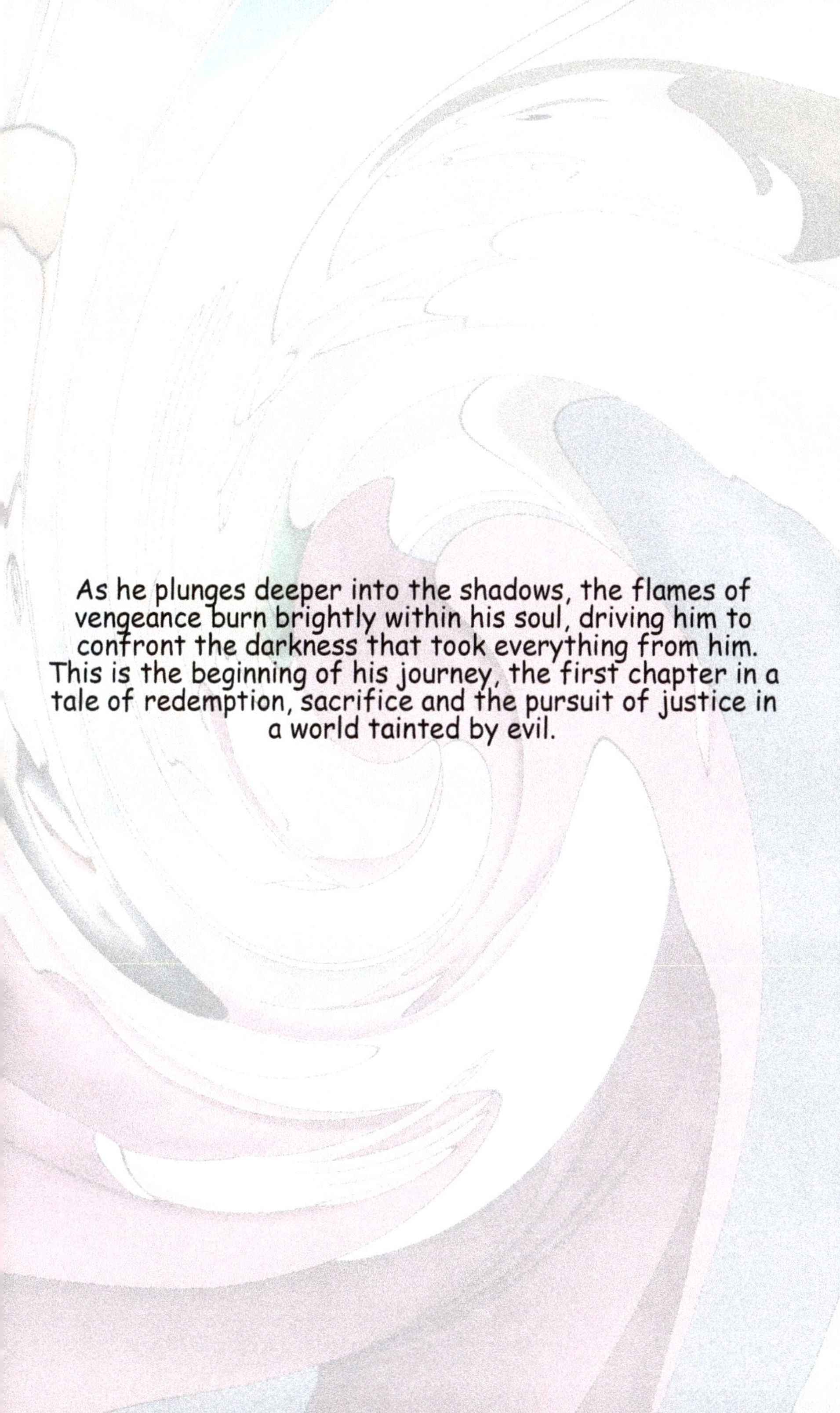
As he plunges deeper into the shadows, the flames of
vengeance burn brightly within his soul, driving him to
confront the darkness that took everything from him.
This is the beginning of his journey, the first chapter in a
tale of redemption, sacrifice and the pursuit of justice in
a world tainted by evil.

Shadows Unleashed

Bruce, now consumed by the flames of vengeance, embraced his new identity as a fearsome antihero. He honed his combat perception, using it to analyze every move and weakness of his enemies. The pain resistance granted him an advantage, as he fought without hesitation or distraction, fueled by his relentless pursuit of justice.

His crime-fighting mastery, combined with enhanced accuracy and precision, made him a force to be reckoned with. Bruce became a shadow in the night, striking fear into the hearts of criminals. His enhanced stealth allowed him to move silently, undetected, as he infiltrated their ranks.

Nevertheless, his enhanced tracking ability truly set him apart. Bruce could follow the faintest of trails, uncovering hidden secrets and piecing together the puzzle of his enemies' actions. With his courage, he delved into the darkest corners of the city, unafraid to confront the monsters that lurked there.

His intuitive aptitude gave him an edge in criminology, deception and psychological mastery. Bruce could read the most subtle body language, analyzing his opponents' intentions and adapting his strategy accordingly. His intimidation mastery, fueled by a chilling killing intent, made even the toughest criminals quiver in their boots.

With martial arts mastery, military expertise and police training, Bruce had the necessary skills to take on any adversary. He moved with deadly precision, delivering precise strikes that incapacitated his foes. His special ops mastery further allowed him to navigate complex situations, always staying one step ahead.

He was also a master of various weapons. Whether it was a combat knife, a firearm or improvised tools, he made use of whatever was at hand to dispatch his enemies.

His opportunity sense honed his instincts, allowing him to seize crucial moments and turn the tide of battle. Moreover, Bruce's power perception enabled him to identify supernatural abilities, giving him an advantage against foes with extraordinary powers.

As Bruce continued his relentless crusade, his name struck fear into the hearts of criminals. The city became a battleground, with Bruce as its dark protector. Though his methods were ruthless, his ultimate goal was to rid the world of those who preyed upon the innocent, ensuring that no other family would suffer as he did.

Nevertheless, as the shadows deepened and the line between hero and villain blurred, Bruce found himself questioning the cost of his vengeance. Would he become the very thing he sought to destroy? Only time would tell, as the story of Bruce Butler Andrews, the tormented antihero, continued to unfold.

A Storm of Chaos

Bruce's footsteps echoed through the desolate alley as he ventured deeper into the heart of the city's underworld. With his senses on high alert, he knew danger lurked around every corner.

On a cloudy Monday night, walking through the streets in a heavy smog. Bruce was passing through the alley that's known as a hangout spot for those linked to his family's tragedy.

Suddenly, a group of armed thugs appeared, blocking his path. With a steely gaze, Bruce assessed the situation, his combat perception kicking into overdrive.

Without hesitation, he launched into action as his enhanced combat skills were put to the test. He engaged in a brutal hand-to-hand fight, with each strike precise and devastating, incapacitating his foes one by one.

Their weapons were no match for his enhanced accuracy and fearlessness. Bruce disarmed them effortlessly, turning their own tools against them; the echoes of gunshots filled the air as he expertly dodged bullets, his movements a blur.

However, the fight was far from over. More enemies emerged from the shadows, their eyes filled with malice. Bruce's martial arts mastery allowed him to adapt to their fighting styles with ease, countering their every move.

His military and special ops training kicked in as he strategized his next move and, with lightning fast reflexes, he utilized the environment to his advantage, using walls and obstacles to gain the upper hand.

The clash of metal and bone reverberated through the alley as Bruce unleashed a flurry of strikes. His killing mastery came into play, dispatching his foes swiftly and efficiently. The streets ran red with the blood of his enemies.

Despite the overwhelming odds, Bruce remained unwavering; his power perception allowed him to identify an enemy with a supernatural ability. Focusing his attention on them, he would adapt their strategy to neutralize their advantage.

The battle raged on, as adrenaline coursed through Bruce's veins. His body moved with instinctual grace, every movement calculated and precise.

As the last of his adversaries fell to the ground, defeated, a moment of silence hung in the air. Bruce stood amidst the chaos, his chest heaving with exertion. The alley was now a testament to his unwavering determination, but this victory was merely a stepping-stone in his quest for revenge. Bruce knew that the city's darkness was vast, and there were still more villains to be vanquished.

With a renewed sense of purpose, Bruce disappeared into the night, leaving behind a trail of defeated enemies. His mission was far from over, and the city became increasingly aware of his relentless pursuit.

Haunted Mind

Bruce's tortured soul found no respite in the darkness. As he ventured deeper into his quest for vengeance, his haunted past began to creep into his present.

One fateful night, as he roamed the desolate streets, his mind was gripped by a schizophrenic attack. The world around him blurred and twisted, as memories and illusions merged into a chaotic storm.

Flashbacks assaulted his senses, transporting him back to the night of his family's torment. The screams of his wife and child echoed in his mind, intertwining with the cries of his enemies begging for mercy.

Visions of fire engulfed his thoughts, the scent of smoke and burning flesh lingering in his nostrils. The pain he no longer felt physically, resurfaced in his mind, amplifying his anger and fueling his thirst for revenge.

Tears streamed down his face as he fought against the onslaught of memories. He not only battled with his enemies in the physical realm, but also with the demons within his own mind.

The line between reality and illusion blurred, and Bruce struggled to distinguish friend from foe. His combat perception faltered, leaving him vulnerable to surprise attacks that materialized from the depths of his fragmented psyche.

Through sheer willpower, Bruce fought through the chaos, determined not to let his demons break him. He mustered all his strength to embrace the present, to push forward despite the haunting specters of his past.

In the midst of the turmoil, a faint glimmer of clarity emerged. Bruce's resolve hardened, his determination solidifying like steel. He would use his pain and trauma as a weapon against those who had brought him to the edge of darkness.

With grim determination, he reigned in his fragmented mind, channeling his schizophrenia into focused purpose. He sharpened his senses, relying on his combat prowess and intuition to navigate both the physical and mental battlegrounds.

As the flashbacks subsided, leaving him shaken but resolute, Bruce emerged from the depths of his own psyche. The scars of his past remained, etched upon his soul, but he had found a way to harness the darkness within.

The haunted memories would continue to haunt him, returning when he least expected, but now, Bruce embraced them, knowing that their presence only served to fuel his determination

Bruce decided he would not let his schizophrenia define him, but rather transform it into a weapon of justice.

The journey ahead would be treacherous, but Bruce was no longer alone. He carried his demons with him, transmuting their power into an unwavering force that would strike fear into the hearts of those who had wronged him.

With this, the tormented antihero pressed on, haunted by his past, yet driven by an unyielding desire for retribution. The battle within his mind would continue to wage, but he would not let it consume him. He had a score to settle, and nothing would stand in his way.

Shades of Betrayal

Bruce's past as a military mercenary cast a shadow of betrayal over his journey. Behind the facade of loyalty, he operated under the radar, executing missions that went against the principles he once held dear.

From the depths of a secret world, he navigated treacherous waters, playing both sides to his advantage. The government, unaware of his true intentions, paid him handsomely for his skills in the information branch of the military while he pursued his own agenda.

Under the cover of darkness, he engaged in covert operations, eliminating threats with ruthless efficiency. The lines between right and wrong blurred as he justified his actions in the name of survival and personal gain.

However, as the years went by, the weight of Bruce's choices began to bear down on him. The faces of those he had harmed haunted his dreams and their accusing stares fueled his inner turmoil.

The unraveling of his past deeds sent shockwaves through his soul, forcing him to confront the consequences of his betrayal. The realization that he had become the very thing he once fought against filled him with remorse and self-loathing.

Haunted by his actions, Bruce eventually vowed to seek redemption for the lives he had shattered. He dedicated himself to a new purpose, using his skills to protect the vulnerable and bring those who exploited their power to justice.

In hindsight, forgiveness would not come easily, as the ghosts of his past continued to haunt him. His newfound mission became an atonement for the sins he had committed, leading him down a dangerous path of self-discovery.

As he delved deeper into his own darkness, he discovered allies who had also been used and discarded by the same forces that had manipulated him. Together, they formed a reluctant alliance, united by their shared desire for redemption and their determination to expose the web of lies that had ensnared them.

Through their collective strength, Bruce found solace in the knowledge that he was not alone in his quest for forgiveness. Each step forward brought him closer to a chance at redemption, as he confronted the demons of his past head-on.

Nevertheless, redemption would come at a cost. As Bruce fought to uncover the truth, he became the target of those who sought to keep their secrets buried. The past he had long kept hidden threatened to resurface, putting his very life at risk.

In this relentless pursuit of redemption, Bruce would be tested like never before. The choices he made would determine not only his own fate, but also the fate of those who went to the same mission years ago he had come to care for.

Shadows of Deception

In the depths of shadowy assignments, Bruce found himself entangled in a web of deceit and betrayal. Sent on a mission to eliminate the cartel boss's brother, he was thrust into a tragic chain of events.

Bribed with a promise of wealth and power, Bruce accepted the contract, unaware of the consequences that would follow. As he tracked his target, doubts crept into his mind, questioning the morality of his actions.

Deep in the heart of the cartel's lair, a fateful encounter would change the course of Bruce's life forever. He confronted the brother, but as their eyes met, a glimmer of humanity sparked within him.

Unable to go through with the cold-blooded execution, Bruce hesitated, torn between duty and his own conscience. In that moment, another figure emerged from the shadows, swiftly finishing the job.

Suspicion filled the air as to who could have orchestrated such a calculated move. Whispers of a rival faction circled, hinting at internal power struggles and hidden agendas.

The blame shifted to a mysterious assassin known only as "The Phantom Blade." With Bruce's reputation for ruthless efficiency and silence, suspicion fell upon him as the one who completed the deed.

As Bruce grappled with the knowledge that he had indirectly caused the brother's demise, he vowed to uncover the truth behind the assassination. This pursuit of justice became intertwined with a personal quest for redemption.

In his investigation, Bruce discovers that his whole branch is a cover up for underground mercenary work Rather than a secret business he and a few other army mates got into, entangling a web of secrets and lies, That he himself got trapped in , navigating treacherous terrain. Each step closer to the truth revealed a new layer of deception, with old allegiances shifting and hidden alliances coming to light.

In the dark underbelly of the criminal underworld, Bruce found himself caught in a deadly game of cat and mouse. The lines between friend and foe blurred as he unmasked the true orchestrator behind the assassination, unearthing a shocking revelation.

The truth tore at the fabric of his understanding, exposing a grand conspiracy that extended far beyond the cartel itself. It was a web of power, corruption and manipulation, reaching into the highest echelons of society.

As Bruce fought against those who sought to keep their secrets buried, he became a beacon of hope and justice. With the truth as his weapon, he aimed to dismantle the corrupt system and bring light to the shadows. However, the shadows of deception threatened to

consume him, testing his resolve and pushing him to the brink.

With each revelation, Bruce inched closer to the heart of the conspiracy, knowing that the shadows held the key to his own transformation. The path to redemption would be paved with sacrifice, but he was willing to pay the price to find justice in a world tainted by deceit.

Shadows Resurfaced

Presently, Bruce finds himself in the midst of a city plagued by corruption and injustice. The scars of his past continue to haunt him, reminding him of the darkness that once consumed his soul.

New York City has descended further into chaos, with new criminal factions rising to power. Bruce, now fully embracing his vigilante alter ego, sets out to restore order and bring justice to the streets.

As he delves deeper into the city's underbelly, he uncovers a web of conspiracies that stretches far beyond what he had imagined. Powerful figures manipulate the strings, creating a sinister tapestry of corruption and greed.

With each encounter, Bruce realizes that the stakes are higher than ever before. His battles become more intense, his foes more formidable, but he remains resolute in his mission, driven by the desire to protect the innocent and make New York a safer place.

Amidst the chaos, a new villain arises, known as "The Shadow master." This enigmatic figure has an intricate knowledge of Bruce's past and seems determined to expose his darkest secrets.

The Shadow Master's relentless pursuit forces Bruce to confront his past and the choices he made. The lines between hero and villain blur as secrets unravel and loyalties are tested.

Bruce's allies stand by his side, providing support and guidance in their shared mission. Together, they navigate the treacherous landscape of New York, unearthing the truth and battling against the forces that threaten to tear the city apart.

As the Shadow Master's identity is revealed, Bruce is faced with a shocking revelation. The villain's true motive is revenge, seeking to avenge the death of the cartel boss's brother, blaming Bruce for not killing the target he was assigned to kill.

The confrontation between Bruce and the Shadow Master becomes a clash of wills, each driven by their own demons. As their battles escalate, Bruce must confront his own guilt and find a way to reconcile his past actions.

In the final showdown, Bruce's unwavering determination and newfound understanding of his past fuel his resolve. He faces the Shadow Master with a renewed purpose, ready to confront the consequences of his choices and seek redemption.

With a mix of skill, strategy and sheer willpower, Bruce emerges victorious, vanquishing the Shadow Master and bringing an end to the reign of terror that threatened New York.

Nevertheless, even as the dust settles, Bruce knows that his journey is nowhere near complete. The shadows of his past will continue to resurface, reminding him of the darkness he once embraced. Yet, he remains committed to his mission, a beacon of hope in a city that needs it the most.

As the chapter comes to a close, Bruce stands resolute and ready to face whatever challenges lie ahead. He is the Dark Knight, the protector of New York and his legacy will endure, even in the face of his own shadows.

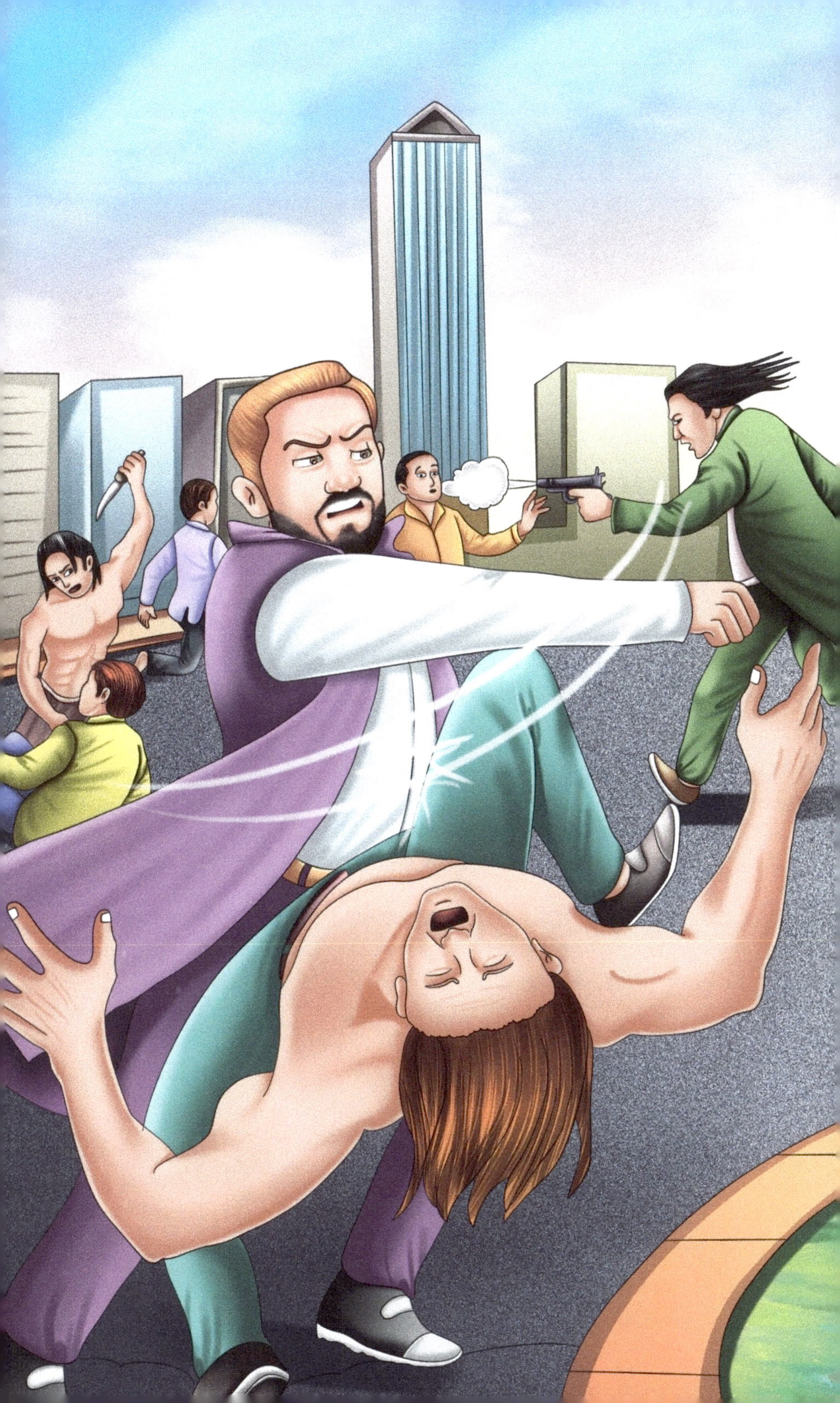

Tower of Shadows

In the aftermath of his victory over the Shadow Master, Bruce embarks on a new mission deep within the heart of New York City. A towering fortress looms before him, a stronghold controlled by the cartel responsible for the death of his family.

As Bruce ascends the tower, the fights he faces become increasingly challenging and intense. Each floor presents new obstacles, testing his skills and determination. He fights wave after wave of the cartel's henchmen, pushing his limits to the edge.

With each passing floor, Bruce's determination strengthens, fueled by the memory of his family and the desire for justice. The battles grow longer and more grueling, but he refuses to back down. The tower echoes with the clash of steel and the sound of his unwavering determination.

As he reaches the upper levels, Bruce finds himself face to face with the boss of the cartel, a cold and remorseless figure. The final confrontation is a brutal clash of wills, a battle that will determine the fate of both Bruce and the cartel.

In the midst of their fierce battle, Bruce discovers a hidden chamber, where a child is trapped, caught in the crossfire of the cartel's operations. The revelation injects a new sense of urgency into the fight, as Bruce fights not only for his own vengeance, but also for the freedom of the child.

The boss of the cartel fights with unparalleled strength and ferocity, fueled by a desperation to protect his empire. Bruce matches him blow for blow, using every ounce of skill and determination that he possesses.

As the battle nears its climax, a sudden twist leaves everything hanging in the balance. The boss manages to gain the upper hand, trapping Bruce in a precarious position. The chapter ends on a cliffhanger, leaving readers in suspense as to the outcome of the battle and the fate of the trapped child.

As the dust settles and the chapter comes to a close, Bruce's ultimate fate remains uncertain. The reader is left eagerly anticipating the final chapter, wondering if Bruce will emerge victorious and save the child, or if this will be his final stand against the darkness that haunts him.

However, as the adrenaline faded, Bruce's body betrayed him. He staggered, his vision blurred and his strength drained away. Collapsing to his knees, he fought to stay conscious.

As his vision faded, a surreal sensation enveloped him. The world around him transformed, and he found himself standing in a peaceful, ethereal realm. There, before him, stood his wife and son.

Tears welled up in Bruce's eyes as he reached out to touch them, but they remained just out of reach.

His heart swelled with a mix of love, joy and sorrow.
In this heavenly realm, Bruce was reunited with his
family. Though he longed to hold them, he understood
that his journey was not over. There was more to be
done, both for them and for the world they had left
behind.

As his wife and son solemnly extended their hands
towards him, Bruce knew it was time to say goodbye.
With a heavy heart, he whispered his love and
gratitude, his voice carried away by the gentle breeze.

Therefore, as his family disappeared from view, Bruce
felt a newfound sense of purpose. He had glimpsed the
other side, the beauty that awaited beyond this world

but he had also seen the pain and suffering that still
existed.

At that moment, Bruce made a vow. He would return to the mortal realm, armed with the strength and love he had found in this ethereal encounter. He would fight for justice, protect the innocent and ensure that his family's memory lived on.

As Bruce regained consciousness, lying among the debris of the battle, he felt a renewed sense of determination. The fight may have ended, but his journey was just beginning. With a quiet resolve, he rose to his feet, ready to face whatever challenges lay ahead.

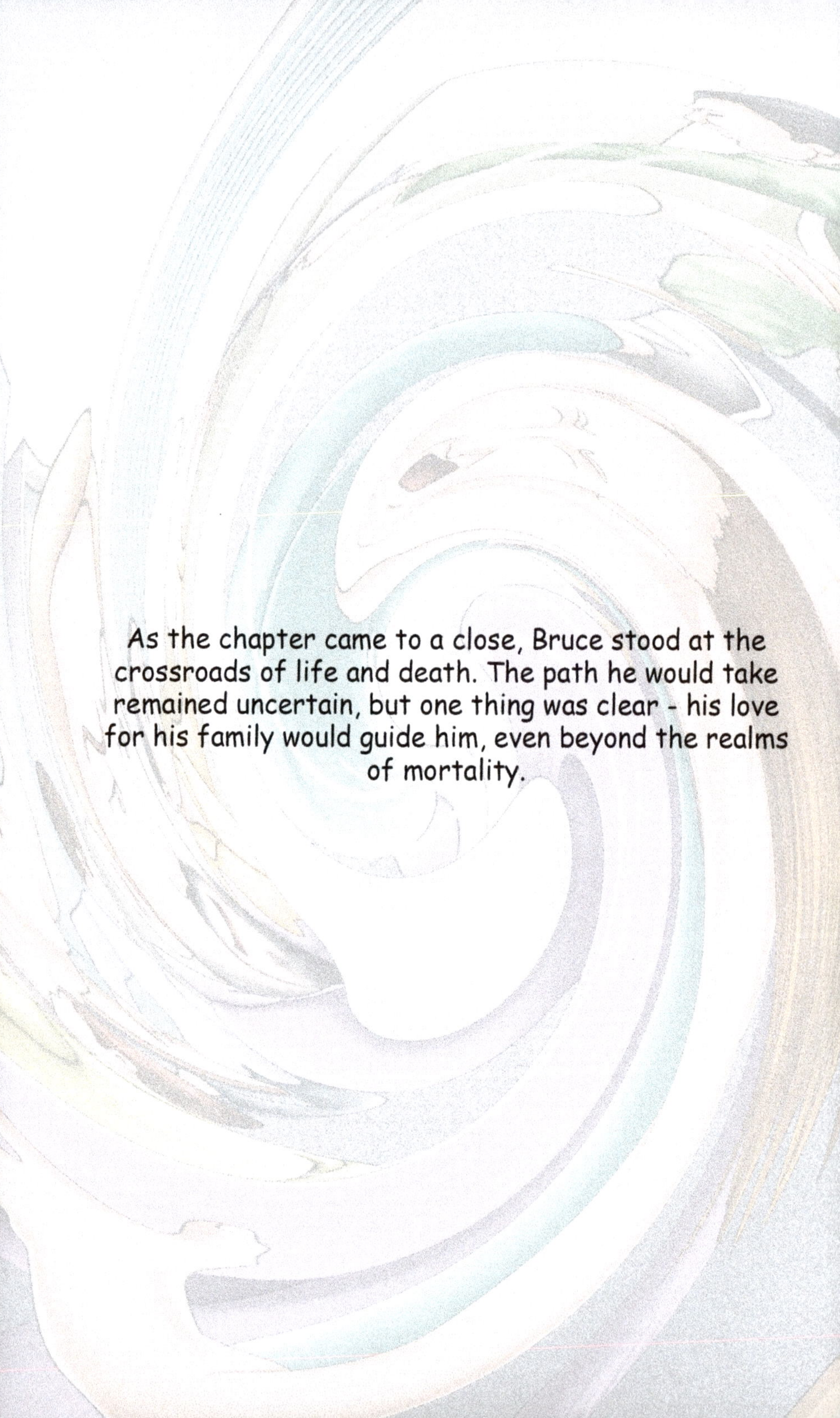

As the chapter came to a close, Bruce stood at the crossroads of life and death. The path he would take remained uncertain, but one thing was clear - his love for his family would guide him, even beyond the realms of mortality.